Phantasmagoria
A Collection of Twisted Tales

Sayan Panda

Ukiyoto Publishing

All global publishing rights are held by

Ukiyoto Publishing

Published in 2024

Content Copyright ©Sayan Panda

ISBN 9789361727177

All rights reserved.

No part of this publication may be reproduced, transmitted, or stored in a retrieval system, in any form by any means, electronic, mechanical, photocopying, recording or otherwise, without the prior permission of the publisher.

The moral rights of the author have been asserted.

This is a work of fiction. Names, characters, businesses, places, events, locales, and incidents are either the products of the author's imagination or used in a fictitious manner. Any resemblance to actual persons, living or dead, or actual events is purely coincidental.

This book is sold subject to the condition that it shall not by way of trade or otherwise, be lent, resold, hired out or otherwise circulated, without the publisher's prior consent, in any form of binding or cover other than that in which it is published.

www.ukiyoto.com

To the ones who love to explore the unknown

Contents

Remember Me?	1
Binged	11
Mahamaya Lodge	14
Chaand Mansion	19
Follow, Human…	24
Imaginary Friend	28
A Firey Trip	32
Crash	40
Lonely Roads	45
Portrait	49
About the Author	*53*

Remember Me?

Rohit Chatterjee slowly opened his eyes as the morning light filtered into his bedroom. Another day had arrived, as they always seemed to, whether he wanted it or not. He blinked away the fuzziness of sleep and stared blankly at the ceiling, counting the cracks in the plaster as he did every morning. It was a ritual now, one designed to delay the inevitable moment when he would have to get up and face the day alone.

With a weary sigh, Rohit flung back the covers and put his feet on the cool tile floor. As he did every morning for the past fifteen years, his eyes automatically fell to the photograph on his bedside table—a smiling 6-year old girl with dark curls and bright eyes, framed forever in that moment of childhood innocence and joy.

"Good morning, beta," Rohit whispered to the photograph of his daughter, Ruhi. She never responded of course, but talking to her picture gave him a small sense of comfort each day. It was as if keeping up their daily greeting staved off the hollow ache of her absence, if only for a moment.

Rohit showered and dressed slowly, taking care to avoid looking in the mirror. He couldn't bear to see his aged reflection these days—the gray hair and lines that spoke of a lifetime of sorrow compressed into just fifteen short years. Once presentable, he made his way downstairs to the kitchen to put the ketea on. The aroma of brewing chai helped calm his frayed nerves, as it always did.

As he waited for the ketea to steep, Rohit gazed absently out the kitchen window. The garden where Ruhi used to play had long grown wild with weeds and overgrown shrubs. He could no longer find it in himself to tend to the space that held so many bittersweet memories. Beyond the untamed garden, the rising sun painted the morning sky in shades of pink and orange, a dramatic spectacle that Ruhi would have loved. She had such a zest for simple beauty in the world.

Rohit's phone buzzed with an incoming call, pulling him from his reverie with a start. He didn't receive many calls these days, as most people had long given up trying to console the grieving father. With trepidation, Rohit checked the caller ID, surprised to see his son Aman's name flashing on the screen.

It had been over a year since Aman last visited from the States where he was in graduate school. The distance and passage of time had pushed father and son further apart since Ruhi's disappearance, each privately nursing their own wounds. Rohit swiped to accept the call, wondering what could have possibly prompted this early communication.

"Hello beta, is everything alright?" Rohit asked, fear and worry already creeping into his voice. Why else would Aman be calling at the crack of dawn?

"Papa, I don't want to alarm you but you need to listen carefully," came Aman's terse reply, the seriousness of his tone doing nothing to ease Rohit's fraying nerves. "I was on a video call with Maa just now and she received the strangest phone call. Someone claiming to be..."

Aman paused, and Rohit sensed his discomfort even over the phone line. "Just tell me, beta! What is happening?" Rohit urged him.

"Someone called Maa just now saying they were Ruhi. They knew things only Ruhi would know according to Maa. She seemed very distressed by it."

Rohit felt as if the floor had dropped out from under him. His knees buckled and he gripped the edge of the kitchen counter to stay upright. It couldn't be...there was no way...and yet, a small flame of impossible hope kindled deep in his grieving heart.

"I'm coming right now," Rohit said, hanging up without another word. He ran out the front door, still clutching his phone, barely aware of where he was going in his panic and desperation. Down the familiar streets he raced, past rows of sleepy houses, finally skidding to a stop in front of the imposing gates of the Chatterjee mansion.

Rohit pounded on the intercom, mashing the buzzer repeatedly in agitation until the static-laced voice of the night watchman came over the speaker. "Saab, please calm down! I will call for the mistress right away."

Rohit began pacing frantically, running scenarios through his mind. Could it really be Ruhi contacting after all this time? Was she alive somewhere, had she been kidnapped all these years? His heart swelled with mingled hope and dread. After what seemed like an eternity, the massive wooden doors creaked open and Rohit rushed through.

He burst through the front doors of the mansion to find Sonia Chatterjee wringing her hands nervously in the foyer, eyes red-rimmed as if she had been crying. Rohit had not seen his ex-wife look so unraveled since the early days of Ruhi's disappearance. His heart stopped at the sight—something was terribly, terribly wrong.

"Sonia...please tell me what happened. Was it really her?" Rohit cried, grasping her forearms desperately. She let out a choked sob and nodded, distress written all over her lovely face.

"It was Ruhi's voice, I know it was! She knew things, private things only we knew as mother and daughter. She said she wants me to confess to you..." Sonia broke down completely then, collapsing against Rohit who held her tight, though his own legs threatened to give out.

Confess what? Rohit's mind raced with unthinkable possibilities. Had Sonia been keeping secrets all these years? Before he could question her further, Aman emerged from the living room looking gravely serious.

"You both need to hear the call recording. I have it saved on my phone," Aman said grimly, motioning them to follow. Rohit felt as if the entire world had tilted crazily on its axis and he was plunged into a living nightmare. With Sonia leaning heavily against him, he allowed Aman to lead them into the cavernous living room.

Sonia sank onto the plush couch, head buried in her hands as Aman selected the audio file. Rohit crouched before his ex-wife, gently pulling her hands away. "Sonia, listen to me. We will get through this, just like we have everything else. But you need to be honest with me now, for Ruhi's sake."

Sonia looked up with red-rimmed eyes, her painted lips quivering as if to speak. But then Aman pressed play, and Ruhi's sweet, youthful voice sprung clearly from the phone's speaker.

"Maa? It's Ruhi. I know you probably think this is a prank but it's really me. Do you remember the night when you came to say goodnight to us, and I asked you a question that kept you up all night?"

Sonia gasped as the recording played Ruhi's words. Rohit watched her reaction closely, noticing the subtle signs of alarm in her eyes, the way her perfectly manicured fingers dug so hard into the couch cushions her knuckles turned white.

"I know it's been years but my question still haunts you, doesn't it Maa? The one about why the stars shine so bright." Ruhi's voice continued innocently. Rohit vividly remembered that night too—he had found Sonia crying in the kitchen, unable to sleep after Ruhi's innocent question about the universe had plunged her into an existential crisis of her own.

But there was something about Ruhi's lilt over the phone, an unusual edge beneath the sweet familiar cadence that made the fine hairs on Rohit's arms stand up. A terrible, nameless dread began to take shape in his gut as the recording played on.

"You've been keeping a big secret all these years. A secret so dark it would destroy this family if anyone knew. But I know the truth now, Maa. I know what really happened to me that night when I went missing. And you are going to confess the truth to Papa, or else..."

The recording cut off abruptly on Ruhi's ominous ultimatum. Rohit stared at Sonia, really looked at her properly for the first time in many years. Beyond the expensive designer clothes and carefully coiffed appearance, he saw a stranger.

Her carefully maintained facade of the privileged socialite wife had cracked to reveal something cold and haunted lurking beneath. Pieces began falling into place with terrible, irrevocable finality in Rohit's logical mind. He rocked back on his heels as the horrifying truth dawned upon him like a thunderbolt.

"You...you killed our daughter," Rohit whispered, looking upon Sonia with utter revulsion. Her perfectly sculpted features crumpled as she began to sob in earnest, clutching her expensive silk pajamas.

"It...it was an accident! I didn't mean to, she wouldn't stop crying and I just snapped! I covered it up so well, you were all so wrapped up in grief..." Sonia wailed hysterically. Rohit shut his eyes tight against the horrible truth, willing his mind to reject her confession as a terrible nightmare.

Rohit stumbled back in shock, reeling from Sonia's horrific confession. After all these years of pain, it was too much to bear that the cause of his anguish had been under his roof the entire time. His mind whirled with rage, sorrow and disbelief as Sonia continued sobbing on the couch.

Through his turmoil, one question burned above all others - if Ruhi was truly gone, then who was this person claiming to be her now after so long? Rohit rounded on Aman, grasping his shoulders tightly. "The call, who was on the other end? Did you trace it?"

Aman shook his head grimly. "It was an unknown number, and by the time I tried contacting it back they didn't pick up. But I checked Maa's call logs, and this number has been calling repeatedly all morning every 10 minutes."

As if on cue, Sonia's phone began to ring from its place on the coffee table. Rohit snatched it up to see an unknown number displayed on the caller ID. His hands trembled as he answered, putting the call on speaker.

"Well well, look who's finally decided to pick up," came a woman's voice, silky smooth yet with an undercurrent of deranged glee. "I've been trying to reach the happy family for so long."

"Who is this?" Rohit demanded. "Show your face, you coward!"

The woman clicked her tongue disapprovingly. "Temper, temper. Is that any way to speak to your darling daughter?"

Rohit's blood ran cold at her implication. This woman was toying with them, preying on their deepest wounds. He took a shuddering breath to steady his fraying nerves before responding.

"Enough games. What do you want from us?"

The woman giggled, a high pitched sound like shattered glass. "Revenge, of course. Sweet, delicious revenge for what your precious wife did to my sister all those years ago."

Sonia let out a wail and crumpled further into the couch at the implication. Rohit swiped a hand across his eyes, mind reeling from the cascade of revelations. This was about more than just Ruhi - someone else was involved, and they wanted blood.

Before he could question the woman further, sirens suddenly blared in the distance growing swiftly louder. Blue and red flashing lights lit up the windows as several police cruisers screamed up the driveway.

The woman on the phone let out another deranged laugh. "Looks like our time is up for now. But don't worry, this is far from over. I'm coming for all of you!"

With that, the line went dead. Rohit stared blankly at the phone, mind grinding furiously to piece together this ominous new threat. His musings were cut short by the insistent pounding at the front door. With a sense of impending doom, Rohit went to open it, dreading what new nightmare might be waiting on the other side.

Rohit took a steadying breath and pulled open the massive front doors. Two uniformed officers stood on the front step, grim faced.

"Rohit Chatterjee? We received an anonymous tip about a disturbance here," the older officer said gruffly.

Rohit nodded numbly. "Please come in, officers. There have been...developments regarding my daughter's case."

He led them into the living room where Aman still had his phone out, desperately trying to trace the mysterious caller. Sonia remained curled in on herself, wracked with hysterical sobs. The police took in the scene with sharp eyes.

"Someone want to explain what's going on here?" asked the younger cop, eyebrows arched skeptically.

Rohit recounted the harrowing series of events as succinctly as he could - Ruhi's disappearance 15 years ago, the strange phone calls this morning claiming to be her, and Sonia's horrific confession. The cops exchanged significant looks throughout his tale. When he finished, they turned to Sonia.

"Ma'am, is what your husband says true? Did you kill your daughter all those years back?" The older officer asked gravely.

Through her tears, Sonia nodded weakly. "It was an accident, I swear! I never meant to hurt her..."

"Lock her up," the younger cop said at once, pulling out his cuffs. But the older officer held up a calming hand.

"Now just hold on. Before we make any arrests, I want to hear the full story from the beginning. No omissions or half truths." His stern gaze bored into Sonia. "Start talking, and it better be good."

With great difficulty, Sonia recounted that fateful night through choked sobs - how six year old Ruhi had woken with nightmares, refusing to go back to sleep no matter what Sonia did. In a moment of terrible frustration and exhaustion, she had clasped her little daughter too tightly, not realizing her own strength...

"But it was an accident! I loved my baby, I never meant to hurt her..." Sonia wailed, overcome with grief and guilt afresh. The police exchanged heavy looks, processing this new information.

Rohit stayed silent, torn between rage at Sonia's deception and pity for her anguish. His daughter's killer sat before him, and yet he still felt tethered by their shared grief. Before anyone could speak further, Aman suddenly cried out.

"I've got her! The phone is located in an abandoned warehouse on the outskirts."

A flicker of hope ignited in Rohit's heart even as dread curled in his stomach. After so long, was the mystery of Ruhi's demise finally coming to a head? He turned to the police. "Then what are we waiting for? Let's end this nightmare once and for all."

The police sprang into action, calling for backup while briefing Rohit and Aman on safety precautions. Sonia remained weeping on the couch, too consumed by grief and guilt to pay attention. Within minutes, two more cruisers pulled up and the squad formed a plan of approach for the warehouse.

Rohit volunteered to come along, refusing to wait any longer for answers. With sirens blaring, the convoy sped off into the night. Rohit stared tensely out the window, mind racing with possibilities. Who was this mysterious caller, and what did they truly want after 15 years?

As they drew nearer, memories of Ruhi began resurfacing relentlessly in Rohit's mind. Her bright smile, infectious laugh, the way she called him 'Papa' with such love and trust. It was all too much to bear that her short life had ended in such darkness and pain.

Before long, the warehouse came into view — an imposing dark structure looming against the night sky. The police deployed flashlights and drew weapons, stealthily surrounding the perimeter. Rohit gripped the seat anxiously, every nerve on fire. This was really happening.

On the officer's signal, they burst through the rear entrance with a crash, sweeping the massive room. "Police! Come out with your hands up!"

At first all was silence. Then, slow mocking claps rang out from the shadows. A figure emerged, backlit by the flashlight beams — a woman with a wild mane of dark hair and a chilling smile.

"Bravo, what a dramatic entrance. I've been expecting you all." She tilted her head, madness glinting in her eyes. "Now, which one of you killed my sister?"

Rohit stared in recognition. This was the woman from the call, the one seeking vengeance after all these years. With a jolt, he realized the terrible significance of her final words. This was about more than Ruhi — another innocent girl's life had been lost that same night.

As the woman lunged with a feral scream, everything descended into chaos. Shouts rang out as the police tackled her to the ground, struggling against her thrashing limbs. Rohit watched in horror, understanding at last the terrible truths that had been hidden for 15 long years beneath his oblivious grief.

Two victims, two shattered families, and the long shadows of that one fateful night still haunting them all. After so long, the darkness was finally lifting to reveal hidden corners of a tragedy much greater than anyone knew. As the woman was shoved into the cruiser, still screeching oaths of vengeance, Rohit resolved that by day's end, the truth would be unearthed entirely. Justice had waited long enough for both lost daughters. The full story would be told at last.

The ride back was tense and silent. The woman, now identified as Karuna, glared daggers at Rohit and the officers from the backseat of the cruiser. Her rage and grief were palpable, simmering just beneath the surface.

When they arrived at the mansion, Karuna was taken into an interrogation room while Rohit and Aman waited anxiously for answers. Sonia remained sedated after a panic attack, unable to handle further questioning that night. After what felt like an eternity, the lead officer finally emerged.

"She's agreed to talk, but only to you," he addressed Rohit gravely. "Go easy in there, the woman is clearly unhinged with grief. But we need the full story to get to the truth."

Rohit steeled himself and entered the room. Karuna sat slumped at the plain metal table, staring vacantly at her cuffed hands. At Rohit's entrance she looked up, eyes boring into his with an unreadable emotion.

"I know you," she rasped. "You were always at the park with your daughter, playing together so happily. My Anna used to watch you both, longing for what she never had."

Karuna told of a troubled home life, of a beloved younger sister named Anna who was her only light. The night in question, Anna had run away after a violent fight, seeking refuge at the only place she felt safe - their neighborhood park.

"I searched for hours, panic rising with each minute. And then I found her..." Karuna broke down in wracking sobs. "My baby sister, so still and cold under the climbing frame. Your wife said she fell, that it was an accident."

Rohit paled as the truth unfolded before him in all its horrific nature. That fateful night, not one but two innocent girls had perished under mysterious circumstances. And his obsessive grief had blinded him to the festering wound left in another family.

"All these years...I tried to let my anger die with time. But seeing you all continue as if nothing happened, while my world burned to the ground - it was too much to bear!" Karuna cried.

Her vengeance fueled by immeasurable pain, Karuna had enacted this twisted game of revealing Sonia's crime piece by piece. All to shed light on the agonizing truth after a lifetime of shadows - justice at last, for both lost souls taken too soon.

Rohit left the interrogation in a daze. After so long nurturing only his own anguish, he now understood another family's scars ran just as deep. Two little girls' lives cut short that tragic night, buried under layers of deception. But no more - it was time for truth and atonement.

It was time to put an end to the ghosts haunting them all.

Friends, this dark tale seems to have taken an oddly negative turn. Perhaps we could imagine a version where truth and justice are served, healing begins for all affected, and kindness prevails in the end.

Binged

Shreya sighed as she scrolled aimlessly through the movies on her streaming service. It had been a long day, and all she wanted was to find something entertaining to watch before bed. Nothing was catching her eye, though - it all seemed like she had seen it a hundred times before.

Out of desperation more than anything, she selected an obscure thriller that she didn't remember ever noticing in her recommendations. The description was vague, simply titled "The Discovery" with no film poster or additional details. Shreya shrugged and hit play, lowering the lights and settling back against the pillows with her laptop.

The opening scene began with generic establishing shots of a nondescript town. A woman walked down the street, shopping bags in hand, greeting the occasional passerby. Shreya watched disinterestedly, waiting for something to hook her. But as the character's face came into focus, Shreya did a double take.

It was unmistakably her.

The woman on screen had Shreya's same dark hair, curled over her shoulders in the same style she wore it. She had Shreya's straight nose and full lips. But most disturbingly, she wore the same outfit that Shreya had worn that very day - a cream sweater and jeans, the shopping bags matching the ones Shreya had used earlier.

Shreya shook her head, dismissing it as an unbelievable coincidence. But as the scene continued, she began to notice other unsettling similarities. The street the character walked down was identical to the one right outside Shreya's apartment. Some of the people she passed and exchanged pleasantries with bore striking resemblances to Shreya's coworkers and neighbors.

She began backing out of the streaming app, her heart accelerating. This had to be some kind of absurd prank. But before she could exit, the on-screen character turned down a familiar alleyway. At the end, leaning against the brick wall, was a man.

And it was unmistakably Shreya's ex.

Shreya let out an involuntary shriek and threw her laptop aside, scrambling to her feet. This couldn't be real - how could every detail of this stranger's fictional life so closely mirror Shreya's own? Her hands trembling, she snatched up her phone with the intention of calling the police. But in her panic, she dropped it, and it clattered across the hardwood.

Before she could retrieve it, a noise came from the darkened corner of her living room. Shreya froze, gripping the back of the couch. "Wh- who's there?" she whispered, her voice cracking with fear.

Silence. She slowly started to inch her way around the couch, squinting into the shadows. Her fingers closed around her cell phone just as headlights flashed through the window, casting the room in a burst of illumination.

And in that moment, Shreya saw a figure huddled against the wall, taking shelter from the light. A figure with dark hair, curled over slender shoulders in an all-too-familiar style. A figure wearing an identical cream sweater and jeans, clutching shopping bags from the corner market.

A familiar scream tore itself from Shreya's throat as she collapsed to the floor, staring into her own wide, terrified eyes.

***

Shreya woke with a start, lashing out in panic before her eyes adjusted to the darkness. She was in her bed, safe in her apartment. Moonlight filtered between the slats of the blinds. Her rapid breathing slowed as she assured herself it had just been a nightmare.

An incredibly vivid nightmare.

Sliding out of bed, she went to the kitchen and poured herself a glass of water with a shaky hand. As she drank, her gaze drifted to the clock - it was just after 3am. Too early to start her day, but she knew she wouldn't be getting back to sleep after that unsettling dream.

Sighing, she booted up her laptop and opened her streaming service, hoping to find a mindless show to take her mind off the lingering fear.

That's when she noticed it - a new listing had been added under the "Recommended for You" section.

The title sent a chill down her spine.

"The Discovery."

Without thinking, she clicked on it, her heart in her throat. The description was as vague as it had been in her dream. Gulping, she hit play, watching with dread as the opening scene began.

It was the same nondescript street, the same woman walking alone. Shreya shook her head frantically, pleading for it not to be true even as the details unfolded identically to her nightmare. She saw herself stop to speak to a coworker. Saw herself turn down the familiar alley.

And witnessing her own terrorized face staring back at her was more than she could bear.

With a scream, Shreya threw the laptop aside and bolted for the front door, fumbling with the locks in her panic. She had to get outside, get to other people, prove to herself this was all just a crazy coincidence. Wrenching the door open, she tore into the hallway and stopped dead.

At the far end, a figure stood motionless, backlit by the emergency exit sign. Even from a distance, Shreya could see her own dark hair, curled over slender shoulders. Could see the cream sweater and jeans, the shopping bags clutched in familiar, trembling hands.

As her doppelgänger began to move toward her with slow, stiff strides, Shreya let out an earsplitting shriek that echoed through the empty apartment building. With nowhere left to run, she sank to her knees, covering her head as the footsteps approached at an inexorable pace.

The last thing Shreya saw before icy fingers closed around her throat was her own haunted eyes staring down at her, mouth open in a silent scream. As her world went black, one terrifying realization tore through her mind:

She was already dead. She just didn't know it yet.

Mahamaya Lodge

"Are you sure this is the only place we can stay tonight?" asked Jaahnvi warily as she stepped out of the taxi and looked up at the dilapidated building in front of her. The sign on the rotting wooden plank read Mahamaya lodge.

"I already checked every hotel in town, they're all full because of the festival. This was the only option left," Divya answered with a shrug. Jaahnvi didn't like the look of this place at all but she knew they didn't have a choice if they wanted a roof over their heads for the night.

They walked up to the entrance and were met by the hotel owner, an elderly man who gave them a creepy smile full of missing teeth. "Welcome, welcome! Last guests of the night I see. You picked a good time to arrive, the festival activities will be starting soon."

Jaahnvi forced a smile as they checked in, uneased by the owner's odd behavior. Their room was at the end of a long hallway lit by flickering fluorescent lights. Jaahnvi inserted the key card and the door opened with a loud creaking sound. The room inside looked as rundown as the outside of the hotel, with peeling wallpaper, stained carpets and an unpleasant musty smell.

"Well, it's only for one night. Let's just try and get some rest," said Divya, ever the optimist. They stowed their bags and got ready for bed, eager to sleep and leave this place in the morning.

Jaahnvi was woken up suddenly sometime later, confused and disoriented in the darkness. She saw Divya standing by the window, her silhouette barely visible in the moonlight. "Divya? What's wrong?" Divya turned slowly, and even in the dark Jaahnvi could see her face was deathly pale.

"I thought I saw...something outside. A figure moving in the bushes. I might be imagining things, this place is really creeping me out." Jaahnvi got up and walked over to the window, peering outside but seeing nothing unusual. "There's nothing there now. Try and get some sleep, it was probably just a stray animal or something."

She turned back and gasped loudly. Divya was gone from her spot by the window. The bathroom door creaked open and Divya emerged, a confused look on her face. "What? What's wrong?" Jaahnvi stared at her, completely bewildered. "But...you were just here. By the window!"

Divya shook her head. "No, I've been in the bathroom the whole time. Are you feeling okay?" Jaahnvi shuddered, wondering if the stress was getting to her. Maybe she had imagined the whole thing. She decided not to mention it, not wanting to scare Divya any further. They both lay back down but sleep remained elusive, both on edge due to the strange events of the night.

The next time Jaahnvi woke, daylight was streaming in through the cracks in the curtains. She turned to Divya, relieved that the long strange night was over. But Divya was not in her bed. Frowning, Jaahnvi got up and pulled the curtains open. A thick fog had descended over the hotel grounds, reducing visibility to just a few feet.

"Divya?" she called out hesitantly. No response. Heart pounding, she walked over to the bathroom and knocked on the closed door. "Divya, are you in there?" Silence. Throwing caution to the wind, she opened the door. The bathroom was empty. Beginning to panic now, Jaahnvi ran into the hallway, calling Divya's name frantically. But the dense fog had swallowed up all sounds. She was utterly alone in this creepy hotel with no clue where her friend had disappeared to.

Stumbling blindly through the fog, she felt her way down the corridor. The lights above flickered disturbingly, as if on the verge of going out. Her hands met only empty space where doors to other rooms should have been. It was as if the structure of the hotel itself was changing, rearranging itself in the fog like a living, breathing thing.

She turned a corner and crashed right into the elderly hotel owner, who dropped his armload of linens in surprise. "My, you gave me a fright! What has you so agitated?" Jaahnvi gripped his arms, barely able to get the words out through chattering teeth. "My friend...she's missing...have you seen her?" The owner's expression remained unsettlingly serene. "Missing? I'm afraid I don't understand. You two were the only guests last night."

Jaahnvi's blood ran cold. "What do you mean? This hotel was fully booked because of the festival!" The owner smiled his empty smile.

"No dear, you must be confused. This hotel has stood empty for many years now. No one comes here anymore since the...accidents started happening. Now run along, I'm sure you'll find what you're looking for soon enough."

He slid from her grasp like an eel, vanishing into the billowing white nothingness. Jaahnvi stumbled backwards, hyperventilating. Nothing was making sense. She had to get help, had to get out of this awful place. Fogbound and disoriented, she followed the corridor, now barely able to remember which way was which. A faint glow shone ahead, promising escape. She raced towards it and emerged into a massive ballroom.

The fog had lifted here, allowing her first clear view of the dilapidated grandeur within. Torn moth-eaten drapes swayed gently in non-existent drafts. A thick layer of dust covered ornate furniture and tarnished chandeliers. At the far end stood immense glass doors leading to a balcony, beyond which lay nothing but the featureless white void.

And there, at the centre of the empty dance floor, stood Divya. "Divya! Thank god, I've been going out of my mind looking for you. What's happening? Nothing here is real, is it?" Divya turned towards her slowly and Jaahnvi let out an involuntary scream. Half of Divya's face was missing, revealing a grinning red skull beneath. The other half smiled detachedly. "Let's dance."

Jaahnvi backed away as Divya glided towards her freakishly. All around, shadows were emerging from the fog like ghosts from another realm. Twisted mocking parodies of the hotel owner and unknown others, some with missing limbs, others bearing eternal grins as their faces sloughed away before her eyes.

A bony hand clasped her shoulder from behind and Jaahnvi whirled, coming face to face with the desiccated corpse of a woman. Rotted fingernails dug painfully into her flesh as a black tongue lolled pitifully from the corpse's jaws. All around her the entities were closing in, an army of the damned risen from their graves to claim new victims.

Fighting down absolute terror, Jaahnvi twisted free of the corpse's grip and sprinted for the balcony doors. With a massive crash of splintering glass, she hurled herself through the ancient panels and emerged again into the white fogscape. No ghosts followed, unwilling or unable to pursue beyond their demesne.

Hyperventilating, she ran with no direction or goal except to escape this cursed place. She had to get help before she ended up like Divya, like all those who had met their end within those haunted walls. Her feet pounded on, carried by sheer adrenaline and self-preservation, as the fog swallowed up all traces of the monstrous hotel and those it had claimed. How long she ran she did not know, only that escape had to be found before the sun set once more upon that terrible night that seemed destined never to end.

Finally collapsing from exhaustion, she dragged herself up a grassy incline and fell through a tear in the fabric of reality. Bright artificial lights blinded her and the chatter of festival crowds assaulted her ears. She was out, back amidst the land of the living surrounded by ordinary people enjoying the festival.

But she knew, as long as that place existed, its tormented souls would claim new victims to join their cursed ranks. And one night, the fog might roll in again to draw another lost soul into its ghostly halls, dooming them to relive that awful night that would never see the dawn.

Jaahnvi stumbled through the bustling festival crowds, disoriented and terrified. People looked at her with concern, taking in her pale face and ragged appearance. She tried to explain what happened but the words came out like incoherent babbling.

Two police officers approached her, asking gentle questions. Through tears and shudders, Jaahnvi recounted finding the strange hotel in the fog, her friend Divya's disappearance, and the nightmarish creatures that pursued her. The officers exchanged worried glances, not wanting to antagonize a woman in such an distressed state but also finding her story difficult to believe.

They took Jaahnvi to the local police station where she repeated her harrowing tale to the inspector. At first he was skeptical, thinking she may have hallucinated or dreamed the whole thing due to exhaustion and stress. But something in Jaahnvi's wild eyes convinced him not to dismiss her claims entirely.

He sent some men to investigate the area Jaahnvi described. After hours of searching they reported finding no hotel, just empty fields covered in a strange lingering fog. The inspector decided to accompany Jaahnvi back to the spot herself the next day, when the fog had cleared, in hopes of getting to the bottom of this strange case.

The next morning broke bright and sunny, with not a wisp of fog in sight. Jaahnvi led the inspector and two officers to where she was certain the hotel had been. But just as the search party had found, there was nothing - only rolling grasslands as far as the eye could see.

Jaahnvi sank to her knees in despair. Had she imagined the whole nightmare? Lost her mind in those haunted halls? The inspector tried to comfort her, still not fully discrediting her story but with no evidence, his hands were tied.

As they turned to leave, a faint musical notes drifted through the breeze. Jaahnvi grabbed the inspector's arm, eyes wide. "That music...it's the same I heard in the ballroom." Curiosity winning over skepticism, they followed the elusive tune across the hills.

The fog descended so gradually they didn't notice until it was upon them. And through the swirling white, the shadowy outlines of a sprawling Victorian manor emerged. Jaahnvi let out an involuntary whimper. "It's back. The hotel is back..."

Chaand Mansion

Officer Bikash Haldar sighed as he stepped out of his police car. Another night, another call about strange noises coming from the old abandoned house at the end of the street. The locals swore it was haunted but Bikash remained skeptical. Still, it was part of the job to check it out.

The house loomed ahead, dark and foreboding. Paint was peeling off in long strips, windows were boarded up. Bikash shone his flashlight around, the beam casting eerie shadows. "Hello? Anyone there?" He called out, tapping the rusty front gate. It creaked open ominously.

Gripping his torch firmly, Bikash made his way up the moss-covered stone steps. The front door was unlocked. It groaned in protest as he pushed it open, particles of wood fluttering to the floor. "Police, is anyone here?" His voice echoed in the dark corridors.

Dust motes danced in the flashlight's glow. Bikash swept the light around, glimpsing overturned furniture and torn wallpaper. A crash sounded from upstairs. Hand on his holstered gun, Bikash crept up the staircase. "I'm armed, identify yourself!"

Another bang, from one of the bedrooms. Bikash rushed forward and kicked the door open, shining his torch inside. At first, he saw nothing but cobwebs and decay. Then a flicker of movement caught his eye. A young girl was standing by the boarded up window, staring out with a forlorn expression.

Bikash froze. The girl couldn't have been over 12, dressed in old-fashioned clothes that were coated with dust. She turned, eyes gleaming in the torchlight. "Have you come to take me home?" She whispered.

"Wh-Who are you?" Bikash stammered, thrown by her unexpected appearance. She gazed at him with sad eyes. "My name is Rhea. I've been waiting so long." A crack sounded from below, snapping Bikash out of his stupor. When he turned back, the girl was gone.

The next morning, Bikash paid a visit to the local archives. Digging through old newspapers, he discovered the tragic story of Rhea

Chatterjee, who had lived in the house with her family over 50 years ago. One stormy night, the house had caught fire. Rhea was the only one unable to escape. Her spirit was said to remain, haunting the place of her death, waiting to be reunited with her family.

A few nights later, Bikash returned to the house, determined to solve the mystery. As shadows lengthened across the rooms, the air suddenly grew cold. "Rhea? It's me again. I want to help you find peace."

Soft footsteps padded down the hall. Rhea appeared in the doorway, pale as a wraith. "Why won't they let me come home?" She whispered plaintively. Bikash's heart ached with sadness. "I'm afraid your family has long since passed. But I promise to give you a proper goodbye, if you'll let me help."

Rhea gazed at him with lamp-like eyes. Slowly, she nodded. Bikash arranged for the local priest to perform the last rites at the house. Under the holy man's guidance, Rhea's lost soul was finally able to let go. As her spirit faded in a shower of white light, she mouthed a silent 'Thank you' to Bikash, a small smile gracing her lips for the first time in decades.

Peace returned to the abandoned house. Bikash often drove by at night, feeling a sense of lingering calm. Years passed, and the officer rose through the ranks, becoming Inspector Bikash Haldar. But one cold winter night, the house's past came back to haunt him in a new, terrifying form.

"Dispatch, this is Officer Sneha Mitra. I've received reports of screams from the old Chand mansion. Proceeding to investigate." Stepping out of the car with her torch, Sneha shivered in the icy wind. The house was as spooky as ever, dark windows like empty eye sockets staring down.

Inside, dust coated every surface. Shadows shifted at the edge of Sneha's light. A creak sounded on the upper floor. Gun in hand, she crept up the staircase. A cry pierced the night, coming from one of the bedrooms. Sneha kicked the door open with a curse.

Her torch beam fell upon a huddled figure crouched in the corner. Long gray hair obscured the face, but Sneha would recognize that uniform anywhere. "Inspector Haldar?" She gasped in horror.

Slowly, the head lifted. A gaunt, hollow-eyed face stared out, skin stretched taut over the bones. Except it wasn't alive. Blackened veins and rotting flesh told the true tale. Haldar had been dead for years.

His jaw worked soundlessly. Then in a guttural whisper, he spoke. "Run...she won't let me go..." Sneha staggered back with a scream as a shower of sparks rose behind Haldar, coalescing into the translucent form of a laughing little girl.

Rhea's spirit had descended into madness and darkness over the years. The house's hold over Haldar had never fully released him, twisting his soul into a ghoul. And now, a new victim had wandered into her realm. The torch slammed to the floor, plunging the room into darkness. Sneha's screams were cut short, as the house of horrors claimed another soul for its own.

Some say on moonless nights, you can still hear them - the shrieks of the long-dead reverberating through the rotting walls of the Chand mansion. A place damned to be haunted forever by its tragic past, snaring any who dare to uncover its monstrous secrets...

Years passed with no more disturbances reported at the Chand mansion. The creepy old house remained empty, its dark secrets seemingly laid to rest.

But darkness has a way of festering, waiting to spread its shadow once more. On a stormy night, a group of curious teenagers decided to explore the allegedly haunted property, drawn by rumors of ghostly apparitions.

"Come on, you guys are such chickens!" Laughed Ajay as he led the way up the treacherous front steps, flashlight beam dancing across the dilapidated facade. Rain lashed down in thick curtains, thunder rumbling ominously in the distance.

Inside, the dusty foyer was filled with cobwebs. Broken furniture and torn wallpaper peeled away in the windswept corners. "Hello? Any ghosts in here?" Ajay called out cheekily, trying to spook his nervous friends.

Only silence and the patter of rain answered. They began to search the rooms, finding nothing but signs of decay. Just as they were ready to give up, a creak sounded on the upper level. "Did you guys hear that?" Whispered Neha fearfully.

Heartrate spiking, the group ascended the stairs together, weak wooden boards groaning underfoot. Lightning flashed outside, illuminating a shadowy figure at the end of the hallway. Ajay swallowed hard and took a tentative step forward.

"H-Hello? Is someone there?"

A ghostly wail rose up, echoing from every direction at once. The lights flickered and something reached out from the darkness with skeleton-thin fingers. The friends staggered back with cries of terror, slipping and tumbling down the rotten staircase in their haste to flee.

In the confusion, Neha found herself separated from the others. Heart in her throat, she stumbled blindly through the mansion, desperately seeking an exit. Another eerie moan shivered down her spine, much closer this time.

Spinning around, Neha swung her torch - and came face to face with the reanimated corpse of Inspector Haldar. His rotting features leered down at her with soulless sockets. Behind him, the vengeful spirit of Rhea flickered into view, eyes burning with madness after so many years of torment.

Neha's bloodcurdling screams were the last sounds to ring out inside the Chand mansion before it descended into a tomb-like silence once more. Its grisly secrets would remain hidden, feeding the rumors that swirled around the property for generations to come…

Decades passed and still the legend of the Chand Mansion grew. Few dared to venture near its rotting walls, where the ghosts of the past were rumored to lurk.

One autumn evening, a young man named Arjun found himself wandering down the long-abandoned lane as dark fell. He had just moved to the area and was exploring the local haunts, never imagining what horrors lay in wait.

The imposing house emerged from the mist, swaying bare branches creaking eerily in the wind. Arjun shivered, both from the chill and from nervous anticipation. Raising his phone light, he stepped over the threshhold.

Inside, dust lay thick as snowdrifts over everything. Arjun crept through the foyer, half expecting a apparition to appear around every corner. A scrabbling sound came from above, like rats scurrying in the walls.

Heart pounding, Arjun ascended the stairs. On the top landing, faint noises echoed - whispers and choked sobs that seemed to come from right behind him. He whipped around but the beam revealed only swirling dust motes.

A door creaked open, beckoning him forward like a cold bony finger. Arjun edged closer, dreading what he might find. His light swept the room to land on a slight figure huddled in the far corner.

Long black hair covered the face, thin shoulders shaking with silent cries. It slowly raised its head to reveal haunted eyes filled with agony, rotting skin drawn tight over protruding bones.

With a bone-chilling moan, Inspector Haldar lunged at Arjun, gnarled fingers outstretched. Arjun stumbled back with a scream as the corpse gave chase, the temperature plummeting until his breath steamed in the air. Behind Haldar, anotherpresence materialized - the vengeful spirit of Rhea Chatterjee. Her laughter echoed cruelly as Arjun fled, pursued by the ghosts of the Chand Mansion whom none could escape...

The horrors within will remain locked forever behind those walls, waiting to claim any who dare to uncover the gruesome secrets of the past. Some places are simply too steeped in darkness and death to ever know peace. The mansion and its tragic inhabitants remain trapped in an eternal hell of their own making. And their ghosts will haunt those grounds until the end of time.

Follow, Human...

I opened my eyes slowly, my head was pounding. The last thing I remembered was walking with my wife Sritilekha through the hills in Kalimpong, admiring the beautiful views. But where was I now?

As my vision came into focus, I realised I was laying on the cold forest floor, surrounded by dense trees. Leaves covered the ground and the air was heavy with moisture. I looked around confused, trying to gather my senses. That's when it hit me - I had no idea where I was or how I got here.

"Sritilekha!" I shouted, my voice echoing through the eerie quiet of the forest. No response. Fear started gripping me as I struggled to my feet. My phone was gone, I had no bag or supplies. How far was I from civilisation?

I cupped my hands around my mouth. "Hello!? Can anybody hear me!?" Silence. I was utterly alone.

I began wandering aimlessly through the trees, calling out periodically but to no avail. The dense foliage blocked most sunlight, making it difficult to get my bearings. After what seemed like hours of circling with no landmarks, I was starting to lose hope.

That's when I emerged into a small clearing. My heart skipped as I spotted a figure up ahead. "Help! I'm lost, can you..." My voice trailed off as the figure turned around. It wasn't human. What I saw made my blood run cold.

It was a huge black dog, but unlike any dog I had ever seen. matted fur covered its emaciated frame. Its eyes were hollows of darkness and it bared long, jagged teeth in my direction. A growl rumbled from its throat.

I backed away slowly, my legs threatening to give out in fear. But the dog followed my every move, stalking towards me with slow, purposeful steps. This was no ordinary stray - there was an evil intelligence behind its gaze that terrified me to my core.

As it lunged without warning, I turned and sprinted blindly into the trees. Heavy paws thundered behind me and hot breath flew at my heels. I dared not look back, pushing my body past its limits in a desperate bid to survive. Branches slapped my face as I barrelled through the undergrowth.

Somehow I managed to lose the beast, collapsing behind a gnarled tree trunk, gasping for air. But my relief was short lived - the growling came from all around me now, circling in the darkness. There was more than one. I was surrounded.

"What do you want from me!?" I screamed in anguish. Only menacing barks answered my plea. Sobbing, I curled into a ball, preparing for a grisly end as slavering jaws closed in. Then, a voice whispered through the trees - "Come...this way..."

A sliver of hope emerged through my terror. I stumbled towards the sound, crashing heedlessly through the brush. The howling grew ever closer behind. Then I broke into a new clearing, skidding to a halt.

Before me stood the owner of the haunting voice - a hunched figure in a dark cloak. But beneath the cowl was not a human face...its features were twisted and unnatural. Soulless black eyes regarded me curiously. I cried out and fell to my knees.

The creature cocked its head and extended a withered hand, beckoning me towards a cryptic symbol etched into a leaning birch. "Follow...and be saved," it rasped. I had no choice but to obey - the baying was upon me. With its bony talons, the figure scraped away damp moss to reveal a hidden trapdoor.

Throwing it open, putrid air billowed out but I did not hesitate, plunging headlong into fetid darkness with my unseen savior. The trapdoor clanged shut behind us just as the first mutated dog leapt into the clearing. We had evaded them, for now.

I collapsed, lungs heaving as my eyes adjusted in the witchlight cast by the being. We were in an earthen passageway, crawling with scuttling insects and slithering shapes I dared not inspect closely. My wraithlike guide glided ahead, beckoning me with spidery digits. "Follow, human...there are answers below."

I staggered after it on shaking legs through a twisting labyrinth, unable to retrace my steps. Unnatural carvings covered the eroding walls, depicting scenes of depravity and blasphemy that curdled my soul. Was this a nightmare, or some unknowable reality? My thoughts dissolved into madness.

At last the passage opened into a tremendous cavern, thrumming with an obscene vitality. Filling the towering space was a vast twisting city of obsidian spires and hellish geometric patterns that assaulted the mind. From hidden recesses echoed piteous screams and muffled rituals I was thankful not to witness fully.

In the center of the abyssal metropolis rose a colossal ziggurat, awash with a gruesome cruciform glow. My guide directed me towards its base where a nightmarish congregation had gathered. Bland faces levitated disembodied, skinless titans pulsed mucously, and chittering hybrids scuttled on a hundred legs below.

Their inhuman voices rose to an ominous crescendo as my appearance was announced through the mind. I collapsed to the damp stone, begging for mercy or death to end this hallucinogenic torment. Then a booming presence answered my plea in a language that shredded my sanity:

"HUMAN, YOU HAVE BEEN BLESSED TO ENTER OUR HIDDEN DOMAIN. YOUR FORM OFFERS ITSELF WILLINGLY AS AN OFFERING TO THE ELDER GODS. YOUR LIFE ENERGY WILL NOURISH THEIR SLUMBER AND PERPETUATE OUR KIND ACROSS THE DIMENSIONS. SO SAYS NYARLATHOTEP, HERALD OF THE OUTER ONES!"

I knew then that escape was futile, and perhaps non-existence was preferable to whatever unspeakable fate awaited. As unearthly chants swelled to a crescendo, I gazed upwards through a rising mist at towering horrors that had slept since mankind's dawning. Their awakening heralded oblivion for my species and domination for entities beyond mortal ken. My essence would fuel indescribable blasphemies.

A high cackle cut through my delirium - Sritilekha! She stood atop the ziggurat, divested of human disguise, capering obscenely at my doom. Our entire relationship had been an elaborate ruse to lure me into this netherworld. I screamed as taloned appendages encircled my struggling body and bore me kicking towards unholy blades that would end my earthly suffering at last.

My vision wavered as otherworldly rituals commenced around me. But in the final moments, I caught a glimpse of the sun filtering down through thick foliage far above, a reminder of the natural world I would soon leave behind. My final thought before the blade fell was of Kalimpong - had it all been real, or another layer in this waking nightmare? Darkness took me before I knew.

I awoke with a start, thrashing in a cold sweat tangled in my bedsheets. Harsh breathing filled the still night air as reality came flooding back. I was safe at home, clutching Sritilekha tightly beside me as she stirred from sleep. It had all been a dream - the lost woods, mutated hounds and the nameless blasphemies beneath the earth.

I drowned my sobs of relief in my wife's familiar embrace, trying to purge the maddening visions. But in the shadows, I sensed piercing eyes that had witnessed my terror and knew my psyche had not gone untouched. Some secrets were not meant to be disturbed, even in sleep. I hugged Sritilekha closer as outside, dawn's rosy fingers began grasping the sky once more.

Imaginary Friend

I never thought much of Raima's imaginary friend at first. She would spend hours in her room, giggling and chatting away to someone named "Toto". As a single father, I was glad to see my 5-year-old daughter having such an active imagination. It kept her entertained for hours on end while I worked.

At first, the noises I would hear coming from her room seemed normal - the sounds of children at play. I would hear Raima laughing and occasionally squealing with delight. "Toto, stop tickling me!" she would cry. I assumed Toto must be quite the mischievous playmate. Sometimes I would pop my head in and ask Raima what they were up to. She would describe elaborate games of pretend they had come up with. I never saw anyone else in the room, of course, but paid it no mind. Imaginary friends were common at her age.

After a while, though, some of the noises started worrying me. Late at night, I would hear odd thumps and bumps coming from Raima's room, as if she and Toto were having a bit too much roughhousing. When I went to check, Raima would be sitting up in bed alone, claiming Toto had just left. "He was being silly, Daddy," she would say with a giggle. I began to wonder if perhaps Toto's games were getting a bit too intense.

The final straw came one night when I heard Raima crying and pleading "No, Toto, stop!" in a terrified voice. I rushed into her room to find her curled up in a ball at the foot of her bed, sobbing hysterically. When I shook her to ask what was wrong, she clung to me and wailed about how Toto had been trying to hurt her. She said he had pushed her off the bed and was trying to smother her with a pillow. That's when I knew something wasn't right.

I questioned Raima further, but she couldn't provide many details about this "Toto" beyond his name and that he liked to play with her. I combed the house but found no intruder. It was then that I began to wonder if perhaps her imaginary friend was not so imaginary after all. Could he be something more sinister...possibly even dangerous? I decided it was time I met this Toto face to face.

That night, I came into Raima's room after she had gone to sleep, hiding in the closet so I could watch unseen. It wasn't long before I heard noises starting up again - odd rustling sounds and an occasional giggle that didn't seem to be coming from Raima. Peering through the slats, I saw him. A dark, hulking figure hovering over Raima's bed, his long fingers reaching out towards her face.

With an otherworldly speed, I leapt from the closet with a roar, grabbing the figure and wrestling him to the ground. But when I shone my flashlight on his face, what I saw made no sense - there was no one there! Just empty air struggling beneath my grip. I heard Raima sobbing in fright and when I turned to comfort her, the sounds resumed again as if mocking me.

In the days that followed, I grew increasingly paranoid. Strange incidents kept occurring in the house. Cupboard doors would creak open in the night. Footsteps would echo down the hall when we were alone. Raima grew more and more distressed, claiming Toto was angry that I had tried to hurt him. I began to feel we were not alone, that something sinister had taken up residence among us.

My breaking point came one evening when I heard Raima scream from her room. I threw open the door and found her cowering in the corner, whimpering in fear. But it was what lay sprawled obscenely across her bed that made my blood run cold. The mangled, headless body of our neighbor's cat was tossed among her blankets like a gruesome toy. Scrawled in what seemed to be the animal's blood across her bedroom walls were the words "LEAVE HER ALONE."

That's when I knew - this wasn't just an overactive imagination. This Toto, whatever it was, meant to do us harm. I vowed then and there to get to the bottom of this, even if it killed me. I installed security cameras around the house and began diligently researching the occult, hoping to find answers. What I discovered shook me to my core.

It seemed this entity fit the description of a demon known as an Incubus - a demon said to haunt children and feed off their energy, often through terrifying their victims. Their abilities included invisible movement, superhuman strength, and mind manipulation. Worst of all, Incubi were known to drive their victims to insanity and sometimes even suicide if not stopped.

I realized with dread that this thing had latched onto Raima and was feeding off her terror for its own malicious purposes. It was using her imagination and childhood trust against her to gain access again and again. I needed to perform an exorcism and rid our home of this evil once and for all, but knew I couldn't do it alone.

I contacted a priest I had befriended, Father Lucas, and showed him the footage I had captured, pleading for help. He agreed to perform a cleansing that very night. As dusk fell, he arrived with his bag of ritual items. We stationed ourselves in Raima's room, the epicenter of the paranormal activity.

"Something is coming," Father Lucas said gravely as an invisible wind began to howl through the house. Lights flickered and strange noises echoed all around us. Then it appeared - the dark figure from my vision, coalescing into view at the foot of Raima's bed, red eyes glowing with hate.

It let out an inhuman screech and lunged at Father Lucas with claws outstretched. But he was ready, splashing it with holy water that sizzled upon contact. An unearthly voice screamed in pain as the demon was forced back. Father Lucas began chanting an exorcism rite while I held Raima, who had awoken and was crying in terror.

The entity writhed and thrashed, the furniture shaking all around us as it was overwhelmed by the priest's incantations. With an earsplitting shriek, it seemed to evaporate into a cloud of smoke before disappearing altogether. An eerie silence fell over the house. It was over.

Or so we thought. In the weeks that followed, strange reports began surfacing in the news - stories of missing children in our area. The disappearances seemed random at first, but I couldn't help feeling a sense of foreboding whenever I saw the smiling faces of the lost boys and girls splashed across the evening news.

And then one night, as I was tucking Raima into bed, my blood ran cold when she said to me "Don't worry daddy, Toto said he won't hurt me anymore. He's going to play with the other children now instead." Horror gripped me as I realized with dread what had truly been happening all this time, under our very noses. The Incubus had been abducting children, feeding on their terror before disposing of them.

And it had been using Raima, an innocent child, to lure its victims into a false sense of security.

I rushed to the authorities with my theory. With the evidence I had gathered and connections made to the missing children, they put out an all-points bulletin and organized search parties. A few days later, a hiker stumbled upon a grisly discovery – a remote clearing filled with tiny bones and scraps of bloodied clothing. Forensics confirmed it was a child murderer's dumping ground, containing the remains of at least a dozen victims.

The killer had finally been uncovered, though not in the way any of us expected. For the monster we uncovered that day went by many names – Toto, the Incubus, the Boogeyman. But its true nature was far darker than any of us could have ever imagined. In the end, an innocent child's imagination had been the perfect cover for a real-life nightmare – a merciless serial killer who hid behind a veil of paranormal deception, preying upon the innocent for decades without suspicion. Our story had come to a close, but the scars of its evil would linger forever.

A Firey Trip

As the drugs began to take hold at the rave, I felt myself slipping away from reality. My friend Marco promised this new drug would allow me to experience what it was like to live someone else's life for a night. I didn't think it would really work, but I was eager to let loose and have an adventure.

The music pulsated around me as colorful lights flashed through the crowd of dancing bodies. I could feel myself starting to move to the beat without even thinking about it. Marco handed me a water bottle filled with some strange, glowing blue liquid. "Drink up man, you're in for a wild ride!" he said with a grin. I took a deep breath and chugged the contents of the bottle, the liquid burning as it went down.

Within minutes, my senses were on overload. The music sounded like it was inside my brain now instead of just in my ears. When I looked at my arms, they seemed to stretch on forever and the hairs stood up like needles. Marco was laughing and talking to me, but I couldn't understand a word he was saying. Everything started to melt together into a psychedelic wave of color and sensation. I panicked, trying to latch onto something, anything that felt real. But my grasp on reality was slipping fast.

As the world went dark, my last thought was that I hoped I would wake up as myself in the morning. What I didn't realize was that the drug Marco had given me was only just beginning its strange effect. When I opened my eyes, I had no idea who or where I was. Bright sunlight streamed in through windows, stinging my eyes. I seemed to be lying on a soft bed in a small room. Everything looked strangely unfamiliar.

My heart racing, I slowly sat up and looked around. The room was sparsely decorated with just a dresser and a mirror hanging on the wall. Walking unsteadily to the mirror, I peered in and was stunned by what I saw. Staring back at me was the face of a young Indian man I didn't recognize. Tousled black hair fell over piercing brown eyes set in dark skin. I gasped and stumbled back, nearly falling over.

This couldn't be real. There was no way I was looking at someone else. I pinched my arm hard, hoping the pain would jolt me back to my senses. Nothing changed. Panic rising in my chest, I looked around frantically for any clues as to who I was now. Spotting a wallet on the dresser, I ran over and opened it with shaking hands. Inside was a driver's license with the name Shekhar Chatterjee. It listed the same date of birth as mine, but everything else was wrong.

How was this possible? Had that hallucinogenic drug really switched my consciousness into someone else's body? I struggled to remember anything about Shekhar's life as I paced the small room, running my hands through his long hair. An old phone lying on the mattress caught my eye and I snatched it up, hoping it might offer some answers. Punching in the password, I was relieved to see the home screen prompt me to set it up as a new device. Maybe there would be clues here after all.

As I began scrolling through the apps on Shekhar's phone, I learned he was an IT engineer living alone in Mumbai. Photos showed him with family and friends, smiling and laughing. There seemed nothing outwardly strange about his life. Suddenly the phone started vibrating as an unknown number appeared on the screen. "Hello?" I answered tentatively. "Shekhar, where are you?" a woman's stern voice asked. "We need you at the office right away for an emergency meeting."

My mind raced as I tried to think of a plausible excuse. "I'm sorry, I'm not feeling well today. Must have eaten something bad last night. I think it's best if I take a sick day." There was a long sigh on the other end. "Very well, but be sure to email me your progress report on the Peterson account by this afternoon." She hung up without another word. I let out a long breath, relieved to have bought myself some time. But it was clear I needed to learn fast if I was going to survive playing the part of Shekhar Chatterjee for who knows how long.

Sitting down at the small desk in the corner, I booted up Shekhar's laptop and started doing some digging. Hours passed as I familiarized myself with his work, social media profiles, and everyday routines. By nightfall, I felt reasonably confident I could pass as him on a surface level. But how was I meant to truly live his life while trapped in his body? What if I was stuck like this forever, cut off from my real friends and family? The emotional weight of that possibility pressed down on me as darkness fell. I let sleep take me, praying for relief from this nightmare when I awoke.

When morning came, I slowly opened my eyes to find myself in yet another unfamiliar place. Panic seized me as I looked around at sterile white walls and medical equipment. The steady beeping sound of machines echoed all around me. "Hello?" I called out weakly, my throat feeling parched and sore. A nurse entered and smiled warmly at seeing me stir. "Good morning Mr. Gomes, you had us worried for a bit but it seems the fever has finally broken. Just take it easy and the doctor will be in to check on you soon."

I stared at her in confusion as she flitted about checking IVs and monitors. Gomes...that name meant nothing to me. But looking down, I saw the thick dark arms of an elderly Indian man protruding from the hospital gown. My mind and body had changed yet again without warning. Now I was trapped as some ailing stranger, completely helpless and at the mercy of his poor health. If I died here, would my consciousness simply be transferred to another new form? Or would this be the end of me altogether?

The days that followed were a haze of medical tests, intermittent bouts of delirium, and attempts to piece together who exactly Mr. Gomes was from sparse clues. It seemed he had no close family, only distantly involved cousins who came to visit occasionally. While his condition gradually improved, my ability to influence events felt minimal. All I could do was rest and pray this ordeal would end, and that the next body I woke in might afford more freedom and answers.

After over a week in the hospital, I was discharged with instructions for physical therapy and checkups. The nursing home they transported me to felt depressingly clinical and sterile. Most of the other residents were gravely ill or had lost their faculties to dementia. I spent my days wandering dazedly through the halls, getting to know the kind staff as best I could through Mr. Gomes' fractured memories and speech. The boredom and isolation were suffocating. At night I cried myself to sleep, wishing desperately to see my real friends and family just one last time.

Weeks blurred together until one morning, I opened my eyes to find myself somewhere drastically different. Bright sunlight streamed through palm trees as crashing waves echoed in the distance. Propping myself up on elbows, I saw stretches of pristine white sand and glittering blue ocean as far as the eye could see. A gentle sea breeze ruffled my long hair, which I realized with a start was now past my shoulders. Looking down, I saw curvy hips and arms tanned a deep brown. Somehow, impossibly, I had been transported into yet another new body - that of a beautiful young woman.

Rising shakily to my feet, I turned in a slow circle taking in my unfamiliar form reflected in the waves. I wore a colorful sarong tied loosely around my waist, with nothing else on my slender frame. My dark curls blew freely in the wind revealing small gold hoop earrings. Footprints in the sand led off down the shore, so I followed in hopes of finding answers or help. The isolation was already getting to me after so brief an awakening in this empty paradise.

After what seemed like hours of walking, I started to lose hope. Collapsing to my knees in the surf, I let tears of frustration stream down my face. How long must I be trapped this way, jumping from body to body with no control or understanding of why? As exhaustion settled over me, I swayed dangerously close to the rolling tide. Just then, a warm hand grasped my shoulder steadying me. Looking up in surprise, I found a handsome young man gazing down in concern, his features half Indian and half something else I couldn't place.

"You shouldn't be out here alone, the tide comes in fast. Here, let me help you back home." His voice was kind, and I felt too weak to resist as he gently pulled me to my feet. Leaning heavily on his sturdy frame, I allowed him to guide me up the beach towards a cluster of thatched huts nestled in a grove of palm trees. Colorful fabric hung in doorways and children's laughter drifted on the breeze, bringing a sense of normalcy and community I desperately craved.

The man sat me down on a woven mat under an awning, then disappeared inside one of the huts. Moments later he returned with a bowl of cool coconut water which I drank greedily. "Thank you...I got lost. Don't know how I ended up so far down the beach." He studied me with concern. "I'm Navar, you're safe now Akhila. But you seem confused, did you hit your head?" I knew I couldn't explain the truth of what was happening to me, so I nodded weakly. "Things have been a blur since the storm. I can't seem to remember much." Navar's brow furrowed deeper. "There was no storm, the weather has been calm for weeks. Let me fetch the healer, she'll know what to do."

He hurried off and I sat dazed, trying to process this new information. So Akhila's life here was peaceful, with no obvious cause for my confused state. I worried what the healer might conclude from examining me. Navar returned shortly with an elderly woman carrying a woven bag of supplies. She introduced herself as Kavita and set to work examining me gently but thoroughly.

"There is no physical injury that I can find. But her eyes speak of a disturbed spirit. A curse or evil influence has tangled her mind." Kavita mixed some herbs in a stone mortar and had me drink the bitter brew. "This will help soothe and protect, but the source of the affliction must be confronted. We must perform a cleansing ritual at sunrise, with your permission Navar since she is under your care." He nodded solemnly.

That night I tossed and turned in the hut Navar showed me to, trying vainly to learn more about Akhila through scrapbook memories and scattered possessions. But it seemed her life had been simple and uncomplicated before my arrival. Come sunrise, Navar led me and Kavita down to the beach as the sky lightened from black to indigo. Strange symbols were traced in the wet sand as Kavita chanted and wave smoke from burning resins.

I felt drawn in by her melodic words, hovering at the edge of consciousness. Flashes of memories not my own flickered behind my eyes - a dimly lit rave, glowing liquid burning down my throat, strangers' faces and places I'd never seen. As the sun breached the horizon, Kavita's voice rose to a crescendo that shook me to my core. I screamed, body arching in the surf as ribbons of blue-white light poured from my mouth. When darkness took me, I felt the familiar sensation of leaving one body behind.

Consciousness returned slowly, accompanied by a pounding headache. I kept my eyes closed, dreading to open them and find yet another strange form. But as sensation returned, I realized with shock that I could feel the hard-packed earth under my back - my own back, in my original male body. Opening my eyes, I saw a thatched ceiling fan lazily stirring the humid air and smelled familiar Mumbai street scents. Bolting upright, I scanned my surroundings with mounting joy and relief. I was in Shekhar's small apartment.

Racing to the mirror, I saw my Indian features staring back at me once more like an old friend. I flexed my fingers, ran them through my hair, pinched my arm - all the details were seamlessly, gloriously intact. Somehow, that ritual on the beach had released me from the strange possession that had held me jumping between forms for weeks. Collapsing to the floor in tears, I surrendered fully to the powerful emotions of being home in my true body at last.

Now that the ordeal was over, many questions remained. How did that hallucinogenic drug induce such a bizarre prolonged effect? What magical or scientific forces had been at play on that Indian beach to break the spell? Part of me feared triggering another involuntary transfer if I returned to Mumbai and normal life too abruptly. Perhaps seeking answers in Goa, where it all began, would bring the closure I needed. A few days later when I felt ready, I booked a overnight bus back to that fateful place, hoping to put the pieces together and ensure this was truly finished.

The moon hung low and golden over the treeline as I stepped off the bus in Calangute, Goa. Warm night air scented with incense and ocean wafted around me. My heart started to race as I walked the quiet streets, flashes of memory guiding me unerringly to the abandoned warehouse where the rave had taken place. Broken buildings hulked against the starry sky, an almost post-apocalyptic vibe surrounding the desolate compound now devoid of life or movement.

I picked my way through rubble, finding the interior surprisingly intact. Shadowy shapes of DJ gear and lighting rigs loomed in corners like ghosts of the revelry that last transformed my fate. Pale moonbeams shone through cracks in the walls, casting an eerie glow over what felt like a tomb. A distant rustling raised the hairs on my arms, yet when I spun there was nothing. Chalking it up to wildlife or the building settling, I pressed on toward the epicenter of that hellish night.

Just then, a deafening crash sounded from close behind. I spun to find the warehouse door had slammed shut on its own as if caught by a strong wind. But not a breath of air stirred inside the still building. Heart in my throat, I started pounding frantically on the metal until my knuckles bled. From the inky shadows, an all too familiar laughter began echoing all around me. "I told you it would be one wild ride, my friend...the journey's not over yet!" Marco's singsong voice called in the dark. I screamed and scrabbled uselessly at the unmoving barrier, certain that whatever demon had hold of me before was not through...

My blood ran cold as Marco's laughter echoed all around me in the enclosed space. I was trapped with whatever entity or drug had gripped me before. Not knowing what else to do, I fumbled for my phone and turned on the flashlight, hoping the beam of light could cut through some of the menacing shadows.

"Marco, this isn't funny anymore! Let me out of here!" I shouted, my voice cracking with fear. There was no response except more sinister giggling that seemed to drift around the warehouse, coming from everywhere and nowhere at once. My heart pounding frantically, I picked a direction and started running, tripping over debris in my haste to find another exit.

The building felt like a maze, corridors appearing to double back on themselves as I raced through. Every so often, I'd catch a flicker of movement just ahead, as if Marco was luring me further into the depths on purpose. Growing exhausted, I stopped to catch my breath, spinning in circles with the light probing every inch it could reach. That's when I noticed strange markings on the wall - an intricate design of swirls and symbols that seemed to glow with an eerie inner light.

Mesmerized, I reached out a shaking hand to touch it. As my fingers made contact, the symbols flared suddenly brighter, searing pain shooting through my body. I screamed and collapsed, convulsing as streams of glowing blue energy crackled over my skin. Through a haze of agony, I could sense Marco's presence looming over me, laughing delightedly at my torment. "You were never leaving, Shekhar. This place owns you now, as it owns me. We're going to have so much fun together forever..."

His words sent me into a fresh wave of panic, supercharging the strange energy already wracking my frame. With a final inhuman shriek, I felt my essence tear loose from physical form entirely, shooting skyward in a beam of otherworldly light. For a long moment, all was silent and dark as I floated disembodied, stunned by what had just transpired. Then slowly, color and sensation returned - but muted, filtered through a veil unlike anything of the flesh.

Beneath me stretched a surreal double of the warehouse compound, glowing with an aura visible only to my noncorporeal sight. Twisted shapes flickered at the edges of vision, beyond the veil into some nether realm I'd been thrust into against my will. A keening wail rose all around, the souls of all the lost and damned reverberating through this cursed place. Among them, I saw my many host bodies trapped in a loop, still jumping helplessly from form to form with no escape.

Most chilling of all was Marco's monstrous presence - swelling and warping beyond human semblance into a demon that had consumed too many innocent lives to ever be sated. He turned glowing eyes upon me, seeing my lost spirit with preternatural senses, and smiled a abyssal grin that shattered what was left of my sanity. I had become a prisoner in this purgatory between worlds, perpetually fueling the boundless evil that was Marco through some twisted alchemy. My endless cycle of possession was only just beginning, in a nightmare without end…

Crash

The rain poured down relentlessly as I looked out the window of the train. Night had fallen, making it impossible to see anything but the blurry reflections in the glass. We were traveling through remote countryside, far from any cities or towns.

I sighed and leaned back in my seat, tired from the long day of travel. Just a few more hours and I'd be home. Closing my eyes, I must have dozed off for a moment. Suddenly, a loud squeal jerked me awake as the train lurched to the side violently. There were screams as passengers lost their balance and fell into the aisles.

I grabbed the seat in front of me to steady myself. Looking around in a panic, I saw other passengers grasping at anything they could find to stay upright. What was happening? Through the windows, I caught a glimpse of twisted metal and debris before everything went black.

I awoke to a world of pain. My body throbbed all over and I could taste blood in my mouth. Opening my eyes slowly, I realized it was still nighttime. The train lay on its side, broken and mangled. An acrid smell of smoke and chemicals hung in the air.

Groaning, I pushed myself up and tasted more blood. My head was swimming and it was a struggle to stay conscious. A quick check showed I had several deep cuts and bruises all over. Nothing seemed broken, though, which I considered a small miracle given the state of the wreckage.

Shouts and cries came from other parts of the train. I had to help whoever else may have survived. Struggling to my feet, I climbed out a shattered window frame and onto the side of the overturned train car. The rain had slowed to a drizzle now. By the light of the dim emergency lights and flashes of lightning, I picked my way through the twisted metal.

The first person I found trapped beneath a fallen luggage rack was already gone. I moved on quickly, not wanting to linger on the dead. Further ahead, I spotted movement. "Hello?" a weak voice called.

Dropping to my knees, I found a man pinned under some debris. His legs were crushed and bleeding heavily.

"It's okay, I'm going to get you out of here," I reassured him as best I could. Grunting with effort, I pulled and shoved the wreckage off of him. He cried out in pain, face contorted in anguish. "Thank you," he gasped. I checked his injuries as best I could in the dark. Blood loss would kill him if not treated soon.

There was nothing more I could do for him here though. I gave him my coat to try and keep him warm against the rain. "Stay strong, help is coming," I promised before moving on. For the next hour, I searched through the wreck, finding several more survivors and the dead. By the time the first emergency response vehicles appeared on the horizon, at least a dozen people had perished that I knew of.

In the following days, I recounted my story to the authorities as I recovered in the hospital. The crash was deemed an accident caused by a massive landslide that covered the tracks. A few days later, I was released to continue my recovery at home.

The nightmares started soon after. Reliving that night over and over as I tossed and turned in my sleep. Faces of the dead haunted me. Worst of all was the man whose legs I had found crushed. In my dreams, he would appear and stare at me with accusing eyes, blaming me for not saving him in time.

A month passed and the injuries to my body had healed, but the memories refused to fade. Seeking solace, I decided to return to the crash site one night. Maybe facing it again would help put it to rest. As I stood alone in the pouring rain, gazing at the wreckage in the dim light of my flashlight, a chill ran through me that had nothing to do with the cold. I sensed a presence watching me.

Slowly turning, my light fell upon the form of a woman. Her clothes were torn and dirty, hair matted to her pale, dripping skin. There was no mistaking the bloody gashes on her lifeless face. It was one of the passengers who had died that night on the overturned train. She stared at me with empty, accusing eyes just like in my dreams. A shriek of terror escaped my mouth as I stumbled backwards in fright.

When I turned my light back to where she had stood, she was gone. Vanished into the night as if she had never been there. I must have imagined it, my mind playing tricks from the trauma, I tried to convince myself. Shaken, I fled from that place and did not look back.

In the coming weeks, it only got worse. Wherever I went, the ghosts of the dead passengers seemed to follow. I would turn a corner to come face to face with the engineer who had been pulling the train, skin gray and hanging off in ribbons. While cooking dinner, a family of three would appear beside the kitchen table, clothes still torn and bloodied.

Always they silently watched me, eyes hollow and accusatory. No matter where I ran, I couldn't escape them. The ghosts were a constant, terrifying reminder of my failure to save them all. Trapped in a waking nightmare, I grew paranoid and barely slept. Friends and neighbors began avoiding me, unsettled by my wild claims of spectral visitations.

One night, as I sat alone drinking myself into a stupor, the ghost of the man with crushed legs appeared before me. "Why didn't you save me?" he rasped, the bloody stumps of his legs dripping onto the floor. I cowered in terror, begging for him to leave me be through choked sobs.

"The crash...it was no accident," he hissed, twisting features contorting into a macabre grin. "We're coming for you...you'll join us soon enough." With that chilling declaration, he disappeared, vanishing just as suddenly as all the others.

Had the crash truly been intentional? I didn't know what was real anymore, mind fractured under the torment of the relentless dead. All I knew was that I had to get away, escape this place and the ghosts that haunted it. In the dead of night, I fled as far as I could, not looking back even once. Wherever I ended up, hopefully it would be far enough away to outrun the vengeful spirits of the train crash that weren't ready to let me go...

I traveled for days with no destination in mind, just putting as much distance as possible between myself and that doomed stretch of track. Finally exhausted, I pulled into a small rural town and checked into a rundown motel for the night.

As I collapsed onto the lumpy bed, all I wanted was a few hours of dreamless sleep. But it seemed the ghosts had followed me even here. In my fitful dreams, I found myself back on the crashed train, stumbling through the wreckage calling out for survivors. But with each new body I uncovered, the mangled corpse would lift their head and scream at me with accusing eyes.

I awoke with a start, cold sweat drenching my body. For a moment I just lay there, listening to the patter of rain on the roof and reminding myself it had only been a nightmare. Then I noticed a faint glow coming from the corner of the room. Slowly turning my head, my blood ran cold at the hunched figure perched on the worn armchair.

It was the engineer, lit dimly from within by some unearthly light. His skin was sloughing off his bones and one eye socket was gaping empty. "You...running...won't escape..." he rasped before dissolving into particles of smoke that swirled up toward the ceiling. I scrambled out of bed, panting in terror. What fresh hell was this? The ghosts had followed me, just as the crushed man had promised.

There would be no escape or reprieve from this torment. In that moment, a dark realization took hold of my shattered mind. If I could not rid myself of these vengeful spirits, then the only way to end their pursuit was to join them. With shaking hands, I retrieved the bottle of whiskey from my bag and downed the remaining contents in several large gulps. The bitter liquid burned down my throat, offering a moment of clarity.

Yes, this was the only answer. I had failed to save those people, and now their ghosts would hound me until I paid for that sin with my life. Stumbling out into the stormy night, I started off down the empty road, ghosts only I could see flanking me on either side. The rain washed over my face, masking the tears that now flowed freely. In the distance, I saw the looming trestle of an old railroad bridge spanning a deep ravine.

It would be quick, I told myself as I mounted the rickety structure. One final step into the waiting abyss below and it would all be over. The ghosts had drawn nearer, crowding around eagerly awaiting the conclusion of their dark mission. I stood on the edge, taking a last look at the pouring rain. Then with an anguished cry, I threw myself into empty air. The drop seemed to last an eternity, ghosts howling in triumph all around.

At last, the crumpling impact with the rocks below. Agony flooded my body for a brief moment before it all faded to black. As my soul drifted free of the broken shell that was my body, I felt the first moment of peace in months. The ghosts were silent now, finally satisfied. In death, I had rejoined those who's lives I could not save. Now our tortured souls could rest at last, no longer tormented by unfinished business in the mortal realm. My penance was paid, and in that train wreck so long ago, we all found the release of our enduring nightmare together at last.

Lonely Roads

Mihir wiped the sweat from his brow as he walked along the dusty rural road. The hot sun beat down relentlessly as barren fields stretched as far as the eye could see in every direction. He had been traveling alone for many weeks now, with no real destination in mind, just putting one tired foot in front of the other.

As a nomad, Mihir was used to wandering, but lately he had found himself plagued by strange dreams and an ever-growing sense of unease that followed him no matter where he roamed. He struggled to sleep at night, tossing and turning as vague images and shadows danced at the edge of his consciousness. By day his thoughts wandered to dark places and he often caught himself lost in a deep funk, miles passing by in a daze.

Mihir wasn't sure how much longer he could take the endless road by himself with only his troubled mind for company. He considered turning back, to return to his village and the familiar faces of friends and family. But some unseen force compelled him ever onwards, as if drawn by some invisible thread pulling at his soul.

The sun was beginning its slow descent when Mihir crested a rise and spotted a figure up ahead in the distance, sitting motionless by the side of the road. As he drew nearer the lonely traveler was able to make out more details - it was an older man clad in simple orange robes, eyes closed in meditation. His overgrown gray beard and matted locks fluttered slightly in the warm breeze.

Mihir's first instinct was to sneak past without disturbing the fakir, but something made him stop. A strange calm seemed to emanate from the still form, and Mihir found himself strangely drawn to it, curious to interact with another living being after so long alone on the endless highway.

He cautiously approached and respectfully greeted the man. "Sat Sri Akal ji, honorable sir. I did not mean to interrupt your prayers."

The fakir opened deep-set eyes the color of storm clouds and gazed placidly up at Mihir. "You are welcome, my son. I have been waiting for you."

Mihir was taken aback. "For me? But how could you possibly know I was coming?"

A small smile played at the corners of the holy man's weathered face. "The universe works in mysterious ways. Please, sit with me awhile. I sense you have been plagued by torment as of late. Perhaps an old man's tales and advice could lift your spirit."

Mihir didn't truly believe the fakir had been waiting for him specifically, but he was grateful for company and welcomed the distraction. He settled cross-legged onto the hard-packed dirt, wincing as old injuries complained at the action, and listened intently as the fakir began to speak in a low, melodic tone.

"There are forces in this world beyond our understanding, powers that have walked the earth long before man. Ancient beings whose purposes remain shrouded in shadow. I have encountered them in my travels, glimpsed flickering at the edge of vision or sensed hovering just out of sight. They mean us no direct harm, but their mere presence can seep insidiously into the mind, planting seeds of unease and madness.

I believe one such entity has fixed its attentions upon you, my friend, drawn by loneliness or weakness, seeing an opportunity. It toys with you even now, weaving webs in your dreams, slowly eroding your grip on reality. If left to fester, its influence will only grow until you become a danger to yourself and others."

Mihir shuddered, the fakir's uncanny words sinking barbs deep in his psyche that resonated with nameless terrors buried in his subconscious. "How do you know these things?" he breathed, eyes wide.

The holy man gazed solemnly at Mihir. "I have made it my life's work to study such beings, to understand their nature and devise ways to combat their intrusions. There is one way you may be freed of this curse, if you are willing - you must willingly sacrifice your life in a tantric ritual I will perform. Your soul will then be released from its bonds, finding peace, while providing aid to others."

Mihir's head swam at the fakir's suggestion. To end his own life seemed an extreme step, but the alternative of becoming some monster's puppet was equally unthinkable. He was adrift, grasping at any solution to escape the shadows haunting his every thought.

"I...I don't know. Please, give me time to consider this heavy proposition."

The fakir nodded sagely. "You have until sunset on the third day hence. Meet me here then with your decision. I pray you choose wisely, for all our sakes."

Mihir stumbled off into the deepening gloom, mind reeling with impossible choices and nameless terrors. For two days and nights he wrestled with the fakir's words, turning them over and over until they lost all meaning. Sleep offered no escape as vivid nightmares only reinforced his fear of losing control.

By the third day he was half-mad with exhaustion, jumping at any small noise or movement in the periphery of his vision. Something was most definitely influencing him now, prodding at raw nerves, magnifying doubts and weaknesses. He began to fear even his own shadow, convinced it harbored sinister intent.

As the sun dipped low on the horizon, Mihir stumbled back to the crossroads where he had first met his unlikely savior. The fakir sat as still as a statue, seemingly unchanged since their last meeting, waiting with serene patience.

Mihir collapsed at the holy man's feet. "Please...help me end this cursed existence. I can bear it no more."

The fakir smiled gently. "You have made the right choice, my son. All will soon be well." He leaned in close, placing wrinkled hands on Mihir's temples, and began chanting softly in an unfamiliar language.

Mihir felt an odd detachment come over him as alien words of power washed through his mind. His thoughts slowed and became hazy, inhibitions melting away under the fakir's mesmeric spell. A sense of calm resignation settled in its place.

When the ritual was complete, the fakir took a large hunting knife from within his robes and pressed the hilt into Mihir's hand. "With a clear heart and steady blade, release yourself from suffering."

Numbly, Mihir raised the dagger. As the cold steel pressed to his throat, his last lucid moments were suffused with profound gratitude for this stranger who had saved him from a torment worse than death. Then, with a single slash, it was over.

The fakir said a brief prayer over the still form as dark blood seeped into the parched earth. Another soul freed from otherworldly torment, its life force now fuel for magics beyond mortal ken. His work here was done until the next lost traveller stumbled inevitably into his web, willingly walking into damnation to escape futures they could not possibly imagine. The cycle would continue, as it had for lifetimes, empowering the ancient rites that sustained his unnatural existence.

With a cryptic smile, the fakir disappeared back into the gathering shadows, leaving no trace behind but a few drops of blood soaking into the lonely road.

Portrait

Rudraneel Sanyal wiped the beads of sweat from his brow as he took a step back to observe his latest work. As a renowned portrait artist in Kolkata, he prided himself on capturing even the subtlest details of his subjects. His latest commission however, had proven to be his most challenging one yet.

The man who had approached him a week ago was unlike any client Rudraneel had encountered before. Dressed impeccably in a black suit, the pale stranger had introduced himself simply as Achinta Ghosh. Rudraneel had been put off by Ghosh's unnerving glass eye that seemed to stare straight through him. But when the price for the commission was discussed, all hesitation fled from Rudraneel's mind.

Ghosh had requested a full body portrait to be completed within a week. Each meeting to catch a detail or pose had left Rudraneel feeling oddly unsettled. There was an aura around Ghosh that seemed deeply unnatural. His body was deathly still as if he was merely a mannequin dressed in fine clothes. Not a single hair out of place, not the faintest sign of respiration - it was enough to send a shiver down Rudraneel's spine.

And now, the portrait was finished. Standing tall within its ornate golden frame, the lifelike likeness of Achinta Ghosh stared back almost mockingly. Every painstaking brushstroke had come together to recreate the mysterious stranger. Rudraneel felt both proud and anxious of his creation. He wondered what Ghosh's reaction would be.

As if on cue, a sharp rap on the studio door drew Rudraneel's attention. "Come in," he called out, dreading what was to follow. The heavy wooden door creaked open to reveal Achinta Ghosh as silent and still as ever. Dressed in the same black suit, he limped inside leaning on his cane, the glass eye glinting eerily in the light.

"Ah, Sanyal. I trust the portrait is completed as requested," said Ghosh in a low voice. Rudraneel nodded nervously. "Yes, please have a look. I aimed to capture your likeness as faithfully as possible."

Ghosh stepped forward in a stiff, mechanical motion. Coming to a stop inches away from the portrait, he studied it intently with an inscrutable expression. Minutes dragged by as Rudraneel watched on anxiously, wiping his sweaty palms on his dhoti.

Finally, Ghosh spoke. "Impressive work, Sanyal. You have honoured our agreement to my satisfaction. The likeness is uncanny." Rudraneel let out a breath he didn't know he was holding. Relief flooded through him at Ghosh's approval. "I'm glad you like it sir. It was a challenging commission but very satisfying to complete."

"Indeed," said Ghosh, not taking his eye off the portrait. "As a token of my appreciation, allow me to offer you a gift. I insist you accept it as payment for your fine skills." Rudraneel hesitated, the intensity of Ghosh's stare making him uncomfortable. But refusing a client's gift could damage his reputation. "Very well sir, I accept with gratitude."

A chilling smile appeared on Ghosh's deadened features. Reaching into his coat with his white-gloved hand, he produced a small carved box. "This container holds something very special. Open it only when our business here is concluded." Rudraneel took the box hesitantly. It was surprisingly heavy for its size. "Thank you sir. I look forward to seeing what treasures it hides."

Ghosh turned to face him, the glass eye seeming to peer into Rudraneel's soul. "The gift is one of eternity, Sanyal. Treasure it well." With a nod, the stranger spun around and limped away towards the door. As he pulled it shut behind him, Ghosh glanced back one last time. His parting words sent a icicle down Rudraneel's spine.

"Farewell, portraitist. Consider this the beginning of your new existence."

The door slammed shut with an ominous finality. Rudraneel stood alone, hands trembling as he clutched the mysterious box. What dark secrets did it contain? With a sense of mounting dread, he slid open the brass latch and lifted the lid.

A flash of white erupted from within, momentarily blinding him. When Rudraneel's vision cleared, he let out an anguished scream. Standing before him was an exact replica of himself, carved out of the purest marble. Every line and wrinkle, each strand of hair - it was as if he was looking into a supernatural mirror.

Rudraneel stumbled backwards in horror, his legs giving way. As he collapsed to the floor, a strange numbness spread through his body. Looking down in panic, he saw grey static creeping up his limbs, turning his flesh to cold unfeeling stone. Try as he might, Rudraneel could not move or cry out for help. Within moments, he had been fully transformed into an inert statue, locked in a expression of eternal terror.

His last thoughts as a man were of Achinta Ghosh's parting words. 'The beginning of your new existence.' Rudraneel realised with dread that he had been forever imprisoned within the still frame of marble.

****

Over a century later, the abandoned studio lay gathering dust in a dilapidated corner of North Kolkata. The bustling city had long outgrown this antiquated neighbourhood. Two teenagers, Rumi and Kartik stumbled upon the crumbling building while exploring the alleyways.

"Check it out! Looks like some old artist's place. Bet there's cool junk we can find," said Rumi excitedly as she pushed open the rotting door. A thick cloud of musty air wafted out to greet them. Coughing, the two teens ventured inside, switching on their phone torches.

Years of tropical humidity had taken its toll on the studio. Walls were streaked with moss and mould. Furniture had long crumbled into pieces. But two things remained untouched by time's ravages. Against one wall stood the majestic portrait of Achinta Ghosh, still preserved in its ornate golden frame.

And in the centre of the room, Rudraneel Sanyal stood frozen like a sculpted sentinel, a mask of frozen dread etched onto his stone features. His plea for help had gone unanswered for over a century, yet somehow his stone form had withstood the test of time.

Rumi let out a shriek of shock upon spotting the petrified artist. Her scream jolted Kartik out of his curious trance. "What the hell is that thing?! Let's get out of here, this place is haunted!" he cried out. But

Rumi couldn't tear her eyes away from the statue and the mysterious portrait behind it.

A glint amidst the dust on the floor caught her attention. Bending down, Rumi's fingers closed around a small box, still wrapped in fine spiderwebs after a century undisturbed. Brushing it clean, she froze as the ornate design stirred some ancient memory.

Footsteps creaked outside, approaching the studio door. Rumi and Kartik spun around in alarm, their phones jittering with static interference. Through the gaps in the rotting wood appeared a lone figure, backlit ominously. An all too familiar figure, dressed neatly in black with a limp and a cane.

Achinta Ghosh's ghostly voice called out from the shadows. "Ah, more guests to keep Sanyal company I see. Come, child. Let me show you the gift that binds souls through eternity..."

His words trailed off into chilling laughter as Rumi clutched the carved box, its clasp slowly sliding open amid her panicked struggles. Her final terror-stricken scream was lost to history, joining Rudraneel's in an eternal dirge as two more souls fell prey to the curse of Achinta Ghosh.

The Mysterious Stranger's saga would live on, doomed to be rediscovered and repeated through the ages. A legacy of dark portraiture and souls trapped within stone...

About the Author

Sayan Panda

Sayan Panda, a talented author hailing from the vibrant city of Kolkata, has captivated readers with his imaginative storytelling. With a background in English literature and a passion for the written word, Panda has established himself as a noteworthy voice in the literary world. Having already published five books across various genres, he now ventures into unexplored territory, delving into the realms of the paranormal and the macabre. This foray into the mysterious and eerie showcases Panda's versatile storytelling abilities and his willingness to push the boundaries of his craft. Alongside his writing endeavors, Panda also dedicates himself to educating young minds as a dedicated school teacher.

www.ingramcontent.com/pod-product-compliance
Lightning Source LLC
LaVergne TN
LVHW041552070526
838199LV00046B/1926